## NOTE TO PARENTS

All children love to learn their favourite nursery rhymes and to be able to recite them to family and friends.

If your child is not yet old enough to read alone let him or her enjoy the delightful illustrations as you read aloud. Point to the words as you say them and talk about the pictures.

By enjoying books at an early age children will begin to develop a love of literature and be more receptive to learning to read 'proper' books later on in life.

# Jack and Jill
# and other rhymes

## Illustrated by Gill Guile

Copyright © 1990 by World International Publishing Limited.
All rights reserved.
Published in Great Britain by World International Publishing Limited,
An Egmont Company, Egmont House,
P.O. Box 111, Great Ducie Street,
Manchester M60 3BL.
Printed in Italy
ISBN 0 7235 4483 2

*A CIP catalogue record for this book is available from the British Library*

Jack and Jill went up the hill
To fetch a pail of water;
Jack fell down and broke his crown,
And Jill came tumbling after.

Up Jack got and home did trot,
As fast as he could caper;
He went to bed to mend his head
With vinegar and brown paper.

Hey diddle diddle,
The cat and the fiddle,
The cow jumped over the moon;
The little dog laughed
To see such fun,
And the dish ran away with the spoon.

There was a crooked man,
Who walked a crooked mile,
He found a crooked sixpence
Beside a crooked stile.

He bought a crooked cat,
Which caught a crooked mouse,
And they all lived together
In a little crooked house.

Ring-a-ring o' roses,
A pocket full of posies,
A-tishoo! A-tishoo!
We all fall down.

There was an old woman
Who lived in a shoe,
She had so many children
She didn't know what to do.

She gave them some broth
Without any bread,
Then whipped them all soundly
And sent them to bed.

Ride a cock-horse to Banbury Cross;
To see a fine lady upon a white horse;
With rings on her fingers and bells on her toes,
She shall have music wherever she goes.

Little Jack Horner
Sat in the corner,
Eating a Christmas pie;
He put in his thumb,
And pulled out a plum,
And said, "What a good boy am I!"

See-saw, Margery Daw,
Johnny shall have a new master.
He shall have but a penny a day,
Because he can't go any faster.

I love little pussy,
Her coat is so warm,
And if I don't hurt her
She'll do me no harm.

So I'll not pull her tail,
Nor drive her away,
But pussy and I
Very gently will play.

Hickory, dickory, dock,
The mouse ran up the clock.
The clock struck one,
The mouse ran down,
Hickory, dickory, dock.

The north wind doth blow,
And we shall have snow,
And what will poor robin do then?
Poor thing.

He'll sit in a barn,
And keep himself warm,
And hide his head under his wing.
Poor thing.

Wee Willie Winkie runs through
the town,
Upstairs and downstairs in his night-gown,
Rapping at the window, crying through
the lock,
Are the children all in bed, for now it's
eight o'clock?